D1537442

HECTOR

Written & Illustrated by

Steve Barnes

Dec. 2013.

EARTH AWARE
K I D S

San Rafael, California

In the jungle lived a hippo like no other you will know.

This hippo's name was Hector. He was striped from head to toe.

Some hippos didn't like him, so they'd call him names and shout,

"You're a zebrapotamus! Leave our herd, get out!"

They'd push him down the riverbank
and roar, "Oh go away!

You're just not one of us!
You're a zebra! You can't stay!"

No one knew the reason why
Hector looked this way.

So they laughed at him and teased,
"Find somewhere else to play!"

He hid among the waterweeds
because he felt he should,

but Hector couldn't hide himself,
not even in the mud.

The hippo leader bellowed,
"You're such a sorry sight!
You're not a real hippo with your
stripes of black and white!"

Hector swam to the riverbed
and alone there he did lie.
He had no friends; his heart felt sad.
It often made him cry.

But in the water he could swim
with amazing speed and skill,

holding his breath for longer
than any other hippo will.

One night as Hector grazed happily, some bullies came to call.

And suddenly, to his surprise, they pushed him down a waterfall!

Hector tumbled down and down
and gasped, "Oh no! Oh no!"

As water thundered all around,
he felt his panic grow.

But he was strong enough to swim
and find his way to shore.

With one last heave his body slumped,
for he could swim no more.

And lying all alone,

Hector drifted off to sleep.

His body felt so tired,

and his sorrow was so deep.

He was awoken in the morning by a stripey crew—

a herd of friendly zebras, who looked just like him, too!

"I'm Marmalade," a zebra said.

"Now, whatever happened to you?"

"I was pushed down the waterfall," said Hector.

"There was nothing I could do!

Because I look quite different

from how a hippo should,

some bullies who are in my herd

did everything they could

to push me out and make me leave,

because I'm not like them.

And now I'm lying here,

and I cannot go back again!"

"That's a shame," said Marmalade.

"But why not join our herd?

Soon you'll see that it's a place

where kindness is preferred . . .

. . . And though you may be different, you'll find that we don't care.

Judging someone by his looks would be just so unfair.

Let's be friends, and we'll show you what a pleasure it can be,

to live life as an equal in one giant family."

So they roamed and ran together
in sunshine and in shade,
Hector's friends in any weather—
the zebras and Marmalade.

Hector felt so overjoyed,
his heart soared like a bird.
For the first time in his life,
he felt part of a herd.

Then lying in the shade one day,

he heard some hippos cry.

Perhaps they were in danger!

He had to find out why.

Some hippo kids were in the river,

trying to swim free,

trapped by hungry crocodiles

and scared as they could be.

The kids were shouting out, and Hector's herd of hippos knew,

the crocs would have their hippo lunch, there was nothing they could do.

Hector realized time was short
and though his lips did quiver,
he breathed the biggest breath
he could and dived into the river.

He swam faster than he ever
had and surfaced with a roar.
The crocs had him surrounded,
so he boomed at them once more.

They began to circle wildly as their hunger made them moan.

Hector threw his head back, yelling, "Leave those kids alone!"

The hippo kids climbed on his back and he swam with all his might.

The crocs were gnashing angrily, and the hippo herd went white.

But Hector reached the shore unharmed, and everybody clapped,
the crocodiles still raging as their empty jaws all snapped.

Excitedly the hippos said, "It surely must be true!
Only a hippo could swim so well and hold his breath like you!"

But then they hung their heads in shame, for everybody knew,

though Hector's skin was black and white, he was hippo through and through.

They pleaded, "Please forgive us,
for all our unkind words.
We'd be honored if you'd be
a member of our herd."

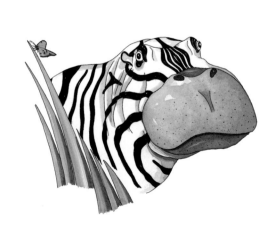

Hector turned to Marmalade
and wondered what to do.
"Where do I belong?" he asked.
"With the hippos or with you?"

"Follow your heart," said Marmalade. "Whatever you decide, you're always welcome in our herd with any color hide!"

Then Hector closed his eyes and thought,
"Where am I to live?
My hippo herd has been unkind,
but it's them I must forgive."

And so he knew the answer,
and it came straight from his heart:
"I do forgive you, hippo herd!
Let's make a brand-new start!"

Hector smiled at Marmalade,
"I'll visit you someday.
You've given me the greatest gift:
a friendship that will stay."

Then he waved and said good-bye
to his friends and Marmalade.
"You're one amazing hippo!"
the herd of zebras brayed.

The hippos cheered with joy, knowing it was true,

that Hector was a hippo, the best they ever knew.

For Sue, Phoebe, and Hermione, with love —SB

EARTH AWARE
K I D S

PO Box 3088
San Rafael, CA 94912
www.earthawareeditions.com

Copyright © 2012 by Steve Barnes

All rights reserved. No part of this book may be reproduced
in any form without written permission from the publisher.

Library of Congress Cataloging-in-Publication Data available.

ISBN: 978-1-60887-070-7

REPLANTED PAPER
Insight Editions, in association with Roots of Peace, will plant two trees for each
tree used in the manufacturing of this book. Roots of Peace is an internationally
renowned humanitarian organization dedicated to eradicating land mines worldwide and
converting war-torn lands into productive farms and wildlife habitats. Together, we will
plant two million fruit and nut trees in Afghanistan and provide farmers there with the
skills and support necessary for sustainable land use.

Manufactured in China by Insight Editions

10 9 8 7 6 5 4 3 2 1

The illustrations for this book were created in watercolor.